VENEFICIA PUBLICATIONS UK
https://www.veneficiapublications.com
Typesetting © Veneficia Publications UK
Additional editing by Fi Woods
October 2020

The Herbarium

A Magical Tale

Written & Illustrated
By

Kathy Sharp

Part One

The Gathering of Strangers

Contents Part One

The Midsummer Summons

At the Hartstongue Inn

Inspired by the hartstongue fern (*Asplenium scolopendrium*), a plant of woodland banks and old walls.

      The rotting thatch contained more moss and fern than reed. In places it had begun to detach itself and was heading earthwards, stealthily, as if the straw might sprout legs and run away back to the marsh the moment it touched the ground. The Hartstongue Inn lay all alone, deep in the forest on an old road that was seldom used nowadays. Inside, the bartender was pretty mossy too, as if the escaping thatch had infectedhim from the top down. Even his hair was green – orwas it merely a trick of the light? Maybe, the pale ferns

shaded the gaps in the roof and swathed everything
within in a green filter. Even the increasingly rare
customers took on a verdant look while they were inside
– a look they carried with them when they left. It wasn't
hard to imagine the regulars having greened over on the
settle and putting down roots, becoming permanent
grown-in fixtures. Would the draped, dry hop-bines,
there as a decoration, not come back to life and grow all
over again? Would the oaken counter, not polished for
many years, sprout buds? Perhaps … and perhaps the
Hartstongue Inn, one day, would be completely alive,
and return to the forest whose clearing it had once so
boldly stolen. Thus, does nature reclaim her own, all in
good time.

But this is all by-the-by because something was
happening at the Hartstongue Inn. If the barman had
been paying attention that spring, which he wasn't, he
might have observed the wise woman tucking a little
scroll of birch bark into a cranny in the wall. Had he
retrieved it and unrolled it, which he didn't, he would
have found its underside covered in mysterious symbols.
They would have meant nothing to him. Butfor the
fortunate few, including you, dear reader, theywould
have transmitted a message. 'Come to the Hartstongue
Inn, or thereabouts,' they said. 'St John'sDay, or
thereabouts.' The bark scroll fell to pieces unmolested,
and its magical message was delivered intothe hearts of
those who needed to hear it. And that was how the spell
was cast to summon the Herbarium.

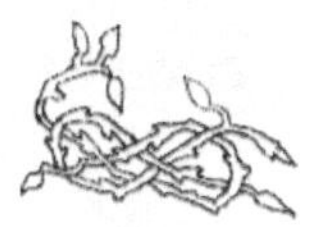

The Wise Woman's Grand-daughter

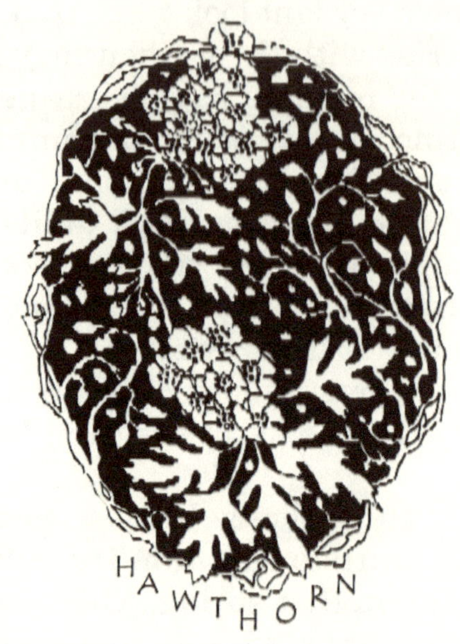

May has her Say
Inspired by the hawthorn, or may blossom (*Crataegus monogyna*)

Some of the people here say cruel things about my grandmother Leonura. They don't say them to her face, but she knows. They say she didn't like her husband – hated him – magicked him into a toad and crushed him under her heel. And got away with it. That is a very vicious thing to say about anybody. A serious charge. But I don't believe it. Others say her husband wasn't my grandfather at all – that there was another man, that he abetted the crime and that *he* was my real grandfather. I think it's just cruel gossip. My mother won't talk about it, closes up like a clam. My grandmother says they were mistaken. No more than that.

Perhaps the truth is that she simply married the wrong man and couldn't regret it when he ran off. But people can't let such things alone, can they? They have to see witchcraft. They love to embroider a story, adding scarlet stitches and gold thread and outrageous images to what is really a very plain tapestry.

The Witch and the Well

Leonura the Wise Woman
Inspired by the motherwort (*Leonurus cardiaca*),
grown for many medicinal uses, especially for women.

'I remember when … when persons such as myself were respected in this village.' She said this with eyes closed, concentration written on her face.

'Oh, my dear! You were never respected – you were *suspected*.' The neighbour who came in to help sweep the house couldn't let this go unanswered.
Leonura opened an eye, skewered the woman with an enquiring look, and then closed up again.

'A tiny distinction,' she said airily. 'They may have suspected things – they were quite wrong of course

– but they respected me, too. Respected my skills. They needed me. I was their healer.'

This was only partially true, the neighbour thought. Had Leonura truly forgotten the accusations that had echoed round the village – round the whole forest? *Could* she have forgotten being held by the heels, head-first down the well? If she'd said the wrong thing they would surely have dropped her. Could anyone choose to forget that? They had called her a murderous witch. It was serious. She was lucky to have survived it. People still whispered.

'They respected me, I say,' said Leonura, eyes still closed.

There was nothing so very respectful about being held head-first down a well. But this new past, Leonura had created in her active mind was full of respectful people.

The neighbour sighed.

'I'm sure they did.' Perhaps it wasn't a good idea to argue with someone who had been tried for witchcraft.

A Midsummer Murmur

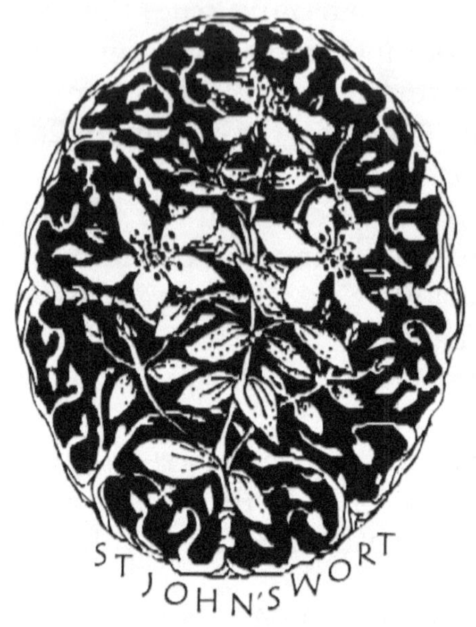

The Sun Stands Still

Inspired by the St John's wort (*Hypericum maculatum*), a plant said to begin flowering on St John's Day (24 June).

It wasn't much of a summer solstice. Sunrise took place by stealth that day, lurking behind a curtain of murky yellow cloud. All signs of rosy pink were lost in *that* particular dawn, and daylight crept out unannounced. One minute it was dark, the next it was grey daylight. Folk were going about their business in the village within the forest that morning in a distinctly grumpy way: feeding hens, raking over vegetable patches. They felt short-changed, as if the summer had broken its solemn promise to mark the midpoint of the year with something spectacular and had then cancelled it at the last minute.

'It's a bad sign. Omen. Can't be right. Shouldn't be allowed.' Everyone felt entitled to a grievance, the right to be offended by an ill-judged weather pattern occurring at just the wrong time.

'Strange things, will be coming. You mark my words!' As always, if it were said enough – and everyone said it – it became accepted as prophetic truth. The gloomy summer solstice became a sure-fire prophecy of unwelcome change. So, no-one was the least bit surprised when, soon afterwards, the strangers began to arrive.

The Philosophical Doctor

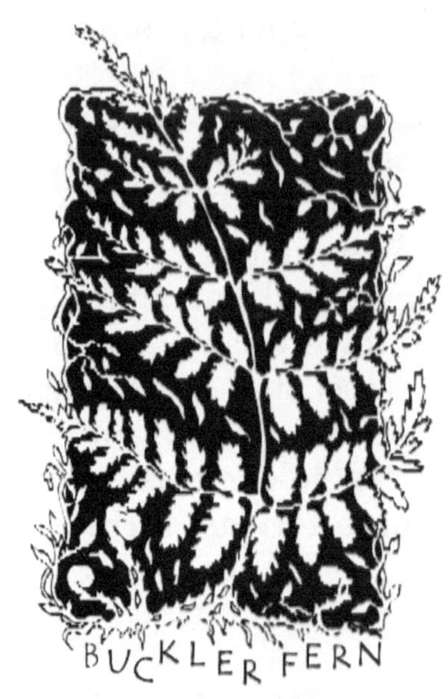

Dr Buckler

Inspired by the broad buckler fern (*Dryopteris dilatata*), a plant of shady habits.

It was a stretch of the imagination to call it an inn. Much of it was in an advanced state of dilapidation, if not outright ruin. The dust-laden windsthat blew through the forest in summer had sandpapered the outer walls rubbing down the corners into curves. People in the village called it the Roundhouse for this reason. Every mountebank thatpassed through the forest, and there were a fair few,seeking takers for their cure-alls and turn-iron-into-gold schemes stopped off at the Roundhouse. Not because they liked it, but because the local folk were notably gullible.

It was a good place to set up your little table and offer your infallible bottled cure for the constipation, thought Dr Buckler as he tramped through the dusty forest. People here forgot so quickly that the stuff didn't work. It was only coloured water, after all. It did no harm – although some of the dyes were of doubtful chemical provenance. Dr Buckler dismissed such thoughts from his mind as he walked. Business was business, money was money and he needed to know where his next meal was coming from. Besides, the gullible seemed to enjoy being cheated, they really did. His quack cures were entertainment in a bottle. People would pour the blue liquid down their throats and announce that they felt better already. It was all mind over matter of course – but who was Dr Buckler to deny them their moment of frenzied happiness and the certainty of an imminent cure? Sometimes, indeed, they truly were cured, though he had no idea how that might have happened. *Ask no questions.* So, on he strode, Barabas Buckler, purveyor of nostrums to the discerning citizen, heading for the Roundhouse, clinking as he walked.

❉

'There are many stars,' observed Dr Buckler, knowledgeably. 'Some people like to give them names, you know.' Tam Ullage, landlord of the Roundhouse, tried to look intelligent.

'So, I hear,' he said. 'Some have very ancient names, I believe. But what happens to the names whena star falls to earth?'

Dr Buckler looked puzzled for a moment, and then recovered.

'Well, well. I hadn't thought of it. I suppose a star's name is lost when it falls. Or perhaps another star steps in to take its place, and takes the name, too. Like a family passing on names through the generations. An interesting question, innkeeper – very philosophical.'

Tam was delighted at the idea of having had a philosophical thought. They were useful things; you could throw one into a crowd of drinkers and they'd need a lot of ale to argue it out. He looked hopefully at Dr Buckler, whose mug was empty, but the fellow (surely not a *proper* doctor) had fallen into a deep contemplation and didn't seem about to order a refill.

Still, Tam thought, I must remember that one. Stars, names of, and what happens to the name when they are careless enough to fall out of the sky. He stored it away in his head for future use. There were always plenty of odd things to think about if you just put your mind to it – and nearly all of them good for the inn-keeping trade.

'Well, well,' said Dr Buckler, coming out of his reverie, 'you have given me much to think about. More of your excellent ale, please, landlord, and then I must go. Important business to attend to, y'know.'

Tam served him jovially. If I'm to continue having these philosophical ideas, he thought, I'd best set up an extra brew. Then they can talk, and drink, til all the stars fall out of the sky.'

The Lady of the Moon

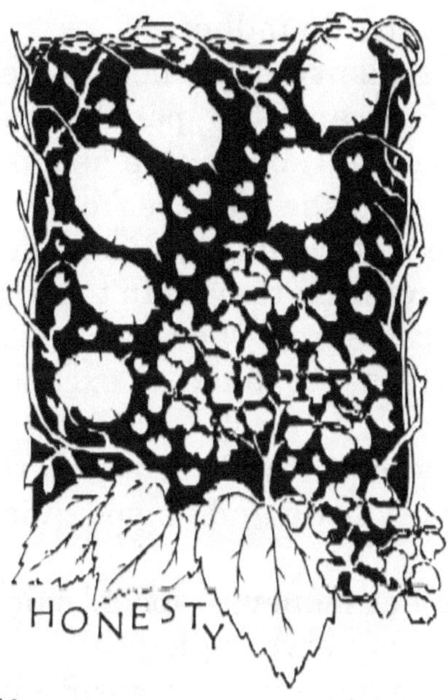

Mistress Honesty

Inspired by the honesty or money plant (*Lunaria annua*), grown in cottage gardens for its beautiful purse-like seedpods.

A thick beam of sunshine, full of dust and dancing insects, fell between the trees, and there she was, suddenly illuminated. She wore a soft violet robe that covered everything but her hands and face; her flesh was pale, her face the shape of the full-moon.

No one had seen her arrive, though the villagers were now vigilant in watching for strangers.

'Don't worry,' someone said. 'I know of her. She is honest enough.'

She was certainly no ragamuffin, anyway; her robe was very clean, and she was fastidious, taking a room to herself at the Roundhouse.

'There was plenty of money in her purse,' observed Tam Ullage, and that, people agreed, was good reason enough to be fastidious. She had as much to lose as they did. Some said she must be from the city. Where else could anyone have come by a robe like that? People nodded, sagely; anything they didn't recognise, good or bad, was said to 'come from the city.' It wasn't a judgement, exactly, but it made an excellent interim explanation.

The lady herself – and they soon thought of her as a lady – said very little and stayed quietly in her room.

'Counting her money, I 'spect,' said a wag, setting off a round of nervous giggles.

All the same her serene presence unnerved them, and they looked forward to the time when she would move on. Though it has to be said they'd have been quite happy to see her leave her purse of money behind when she left.

The Bearded Lady

Ursula Borage

Inspired by the borage (*Borago officinalis*), a pretty herb whose name derives from a word meaning 'hairy'.

'She has a better beard than her husband!'
Somebody said it loud enough for her to hear.
'Does she have a husband, then?' another voice asked.
'If she has, she outdoes him in beard!'
Cruel sniggering followed, all concealed behind hands, but not suppressed. She was meant to hear.

Behind the beard, she smiled. It had its uses. And she flicked her fingers at the group of villagers, asif to see off a troublesome fly. She couldn't help the beard; it had just appeared with womanhood, and, iftruth be told, she didn't mind it. The jibes had alwaysbeen cruel, of course, but her hairiness had formed a protective barrier over time, and these days the sly insults, and the not so sly, simply bounced off. She was no more harmed by them than a bear by the impact of a raindrop on its pelt. Her fingers, darkly hairy to the knuckle, flicked them away again.

'Just wait,' she said into the lustrous beard, 'just wait until winter comes, and you are wheezing and snotting your way through the frost.'

Her eyes, true blue, flickered at the thought. Deep down there was a little giggle at the expense of her tormentors. They would change their tune when the winter got its knotty hands on their lungs and made gathering their firewood a torture.

They would anticipate her arrival in the forest – call on her for cures. And never mention the beard at all.

No, she didn't mind the beard – it was the mark of her trade. Consult the bearded lady, they would say, she cures the pleurisy. There would be no jibes in the winter. She smiled again into the beard and trudged on, heading for the Hartstongue Inn.

The Unlucky Man

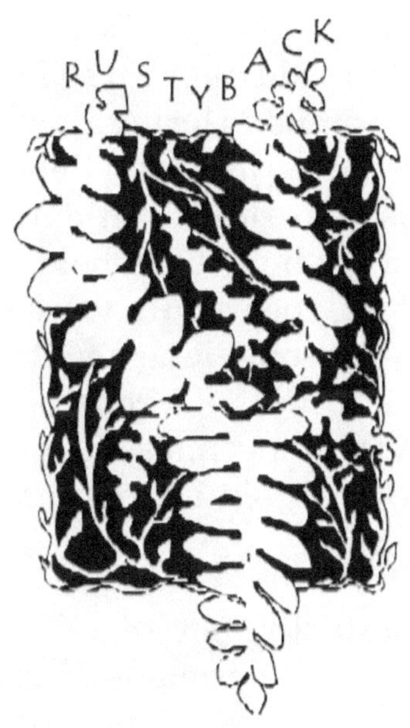

Old Rustyback

Inspired by the rustyback fern (*Asplenium ceterach*), a plant of old walls.

Fast asleep he resembled a heap of rubbish. Or perhaps a sweeping of dead leaves. It was all down to the cloak; it had once been a sumptuous russet-coloured velvet, silk lined, and very valuable. Only a person of great wealth could have purchased it, possessed it, and worn it with panache. But the years had rendered its plush surface flat, polished it smooth, and the fabulous cloak had been passed from hand to hand, each less wealthy, less respectable, and more grubby, till at last it became the regular outfit of Old Rustyback, as they called him. He and the once-proud cloak seemed to be a single entity these days.

Vestiges of the silk lining, long since worn to ribbons, could have been found, if anyone had wished to look inside, which they didn't. Who would want to get *that* close to a smelly old vagrant? Most people left him well alone as he tramped through town and country in his rusty cloak, which still kept a degree of weather off.

But perhaps a little investigation might have paid dividends, had anybody been bold enough to try it. Neither the townsfolk, the woodlanders nor the old man himself knew that someone, long ago, had sewn a collection of coins into the generous hems of the cloak for safekeeping. And sometimes, just sometimes, Old Rustyback left a trail of gold behind him.

He is an unlucky person, Old Rustyback. He knows it. He has always been unlucky in his choices, starting with a poor choice of parents. Luck leapfrogs over him, takes a roundabout route to avoid him, and laughs behind his back. There is more truth in this than he knows. For once, just once, he *had* made a lucky choice, just by chance, when he picked up the old rusty cloak. He carries that fatal luck with him, sleeps under it, curses it sometimes, and knows not that it leaks away with the failing stitch-work. Gold coins. But someone else does and follows at leisure.

The Ragged Man

Timothy Burdock

Inspired by the burdock (*Arctium minus*), a robust and tenacious hanger-on with many uses, including as a hair-restorer.

When the very ragged man came into the Roundhouse, Tam Ullage, innkeeper, eyed him with suspicion. Tam found, in his line of work, that it paid to be suspicious. Healthy, like. His suspicion levels cranked up when the creature laid a small gold coin before him. Tam checked it for authenticity. It was indeed gold, and he wanted it badly. But suspicion won the day.

'Now how would the likes of *you,* be coming by the likes of *that?*' he asked. It was a rhetorical question and he didn't expect an honest answer.

'I didn't steal it, if that's what you're thinking,' said the creature, standing up straight and looking Tam directly in the eye. 'I found it in the forest. Finders, keepers. Now do you want my money or not?'

Tam counted himself a good judge of character, and to his surprise his judgement told him this was an honest answer. He looked longingly at the coin. It would look very well with the others – his little stash of gold, growing slowly, that would one day take him out of this god-forsaken place and off to the city.

On the other hand, if this coin had actually been stolen, Tam didn't want anyone knocking on his door and making awkward enquiries.

The ragged man waited, looking Tam clearly in the eye throughout, watching the thoughts cloud and uncloud his face. 'Not stolen. Found,' he said again. 'You could buy yourself a very fine horsehair wig with that, you know.'

Tam's hand went involuntarily to the smooth dome of his head.

'All I ask for that coin is a good meal and some ale,' said the ragged man, with an air of being very reasonable. 'No more – and it's yours.'

Tam gave in. 'Take a seat,' he said.

While the ragged man ate, Tam tussled with a dilemma. He wanted the coin for his collection – but he so wanted a fine horsehair wig, too. Clearly, he could not have both. Every time he thought of it his hand clamped onto his bald head.

The stranger watched thoughtfully. When the meal was finished he said, 'Very fine, landlord, very fine.' After a pause he added, 'Perhaps y'don't wish to spend so much on a wig?'

Tam stared, his lips framing a question.

'Perhaps,' said the stranger, 'you'd rather have your own hair back.'

'What d'you mean?' said Tam, all ears.

'I mean it is my stock in trade. Hair restorer. Ina bottle.'

'Ha,' said Tam, 'and I s'pose you want the gold coin back for it, do you?' He hadn't been born yesterday.

'No indeed. I want some small change for it. No more. A few small coins.' And the ragged man drew a bottle of mauvish liquid out of an inner pocket.

Tam looked at it. His own hair! In a bottle! A few small coins. And the gold coin safely in his stash. Both desires satisfied in one easy payment.

'Wait,' he said, and looked furtively in his pockets, all suspicion having fled out of the window. 'Wait.'

The handful of coins Tam threw on the table in his haste was a little larger than he had intended.

'That will do nicely,' said the stranger, gathering them up. 'Drink a spoonful a day, no more, no less; it will make your hair grow in a fortnight, I absolutely guarantee it.' This last was said with another unmistakably honest look.

Tam took the bottle. 'I thank'ee,' he said, his other hand rushing again to his bald pate as if the medicine, by mere proximity, might have started to work already.

The ragged man got up. 'I'll take my leave now, landlord. One spoon a day.' And he walked slowly out of the inn.

Tam was pleased with himself. Why for the cost of a meal and some small change he had both the gold coin and the baldness cure. A superb bargain. He rushed off to find a spoon and begin the treatment immediately.

Mr Timothy Burdock, ragged or not, melting into the trees in the direction of the Hartstongue Inn, was also pleased. He had indeed found the coin in the forest – but for a person such as himself, any attempt to spenda gold coin brought suspicion of thievery, as the innkeeper had just proved. And if the true owner camelooking, he didn't wish to be found with it on his person.He was better off without it. In return he had gothimself a good meal and a large pocketful of small coinsthat he could spend freely without questions beingasked. And all by telling the exact truth.

Every word he had said was precisely true. He had neglected to add, however, that when the innkeeper's hair did grow – and it would, profusely, ina week or two – it would be from Tam's nose and ears, instead of his head, which would stubbornly remain as bald as an egg. But Mr Burdock would have concluded his business in these parts and be long gone by then. He smiled to himself and walked on.

The Man who Cured a King

Mr Knitbone

Inspired by the comfrey (*Symphytum officinale*), a herb with many uses, including mending fractures.

'I'd rather have the broken bone, myself,' said someone at the back of the little crowd of villagers. An infectious giggle began to spread, and it seemed for a moment that the attention of the people hung in the balance.

Please, muttered the man in the middle, to any deity who might be listening, *please don't let them disperse, and with nothing sold yet!* He was a short man in a tall hat – the best he could do in a crowd, even a little crowd – and he called out in a high voice, a little desperate. 'Cures guaranteed, folks! The dried herb or the infusion – choose which you like. They are equally efficacious.'

'Efficacious!' echoed a laughing voice at the back. 'Efficacious, indeed!' The small man ignored this as best he could and went on, 'It's the very thing to have in your medicine chest. Even the king keeps it, you know. Swears by it.'

'And how would you be knowing what the king swears by?' someone asked. The laughter was getting raucously out of hand. The small man, in danger of losing their attention, spoke again. 'The king broke a bone in his leg. Hunting accident. Most severe. It is well-known – everybody know about it.'

There were some nods of agreement this time. The small man saw his opportunity, 'Yes, and it was the comfrey-cure that knitted the bone. All good as new. The king insists upon it.' He was getting back into his stride now. 'And you, too, can have that very same cure – the same as the king himself – for just one tiny coin. It could save the pain and embarrassment of a crooked leg, or a withered arm. Just think of it!'

'But what about the smell, Mr Knitbone?' someone asked. 'Smells something rotten, it does.'

The small man was ready this time. 'All good cures smell strong,' he said with absolute certainty. 'Nothing weak and watery about this one. Good strong stuff.'

'He's right! Somebody shouted. 'I'll have two bottles!' Mr Knitbone smiled, relieved and happy.

'Who's next?' he called, pocketing the coins.

A Man of Letters

The Monk

Inspired by the monkshood (*Aconitum napellus*), a stately plant containing intense poisons.

He wasn't old, the monk, as far as you could tell, but he had a strangely preserved look about him as if he'd just crawled out of a bog after a thousand-year residence. Some people turned away from his shrunken face in embarrassment. He had a redeeming feature, though – he could read and write, and he peddled this useful accomplishment from village to village, making sense of agreements that were no more than scratches on parchment to the average person: interpreting, clarifying, and advising. When it was all done he would show you where to make your mark and take a small payment in cash or kind.

Actual books were a rare thing, of course, and not for the likes of the grubby-fingered public, but the monk brought with him scraps of parchment so he could earn a crust by giving little exhibitions of his writing skills. Sometimes he wrote directly on the ground with a stick, and people would treat the writing as precious and walk around it until the weather faded it or washed it away. In truth, nobody knew what it said or indeed, if it was real writing. But they revered it anyway and considered it lucky long after the monk himself had moved on.

This, then, is why everyone was so surprised that day when the monk wrote on the ground in his usual way – and someone stepped out of the hushed crowd and said, 'No, no, no. You can't possibly spell it like that!'

The monk looked intently at this person, concluded the comment was purely mischievous, and said, 'Spelling is an art, not a science.' And he continued to write, quite unconcerned.

The Quicksilver Man

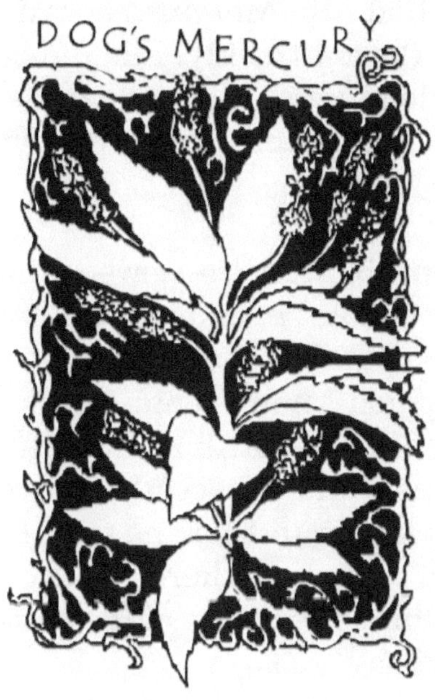

Mercurio

Inspired by the dog's mercury (*Mercurialis perennis*), a poisonous, early-flowering plant of old woodland.

There had been some strange people in the neighbourhood lately. All the villagers had remarked upon it. Among them were regular visitors who were always welcome.

This particular visitor fell into that category. He took his stance on a convenient tree stump, his dog beside him and giving every indication of hanging onto his every word, as he made his announcements. People did stop and listen to him – not because he had anything intriguing to say – but because he was so interesting to look at. They called him Mercurio because his long silver-grey hair flowed thickly, like quicksilver, plus he was an adaptable person. Mercurio understands theway we do things here, people said approvingly. He always fits in.

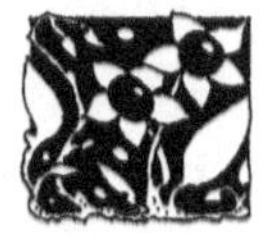

This adaptable nature served him well. He had cures to peddle, of course, as most of the strangers did, but the villagers were good-natured with him and bought bottles of god-knows-what on his assurance thatit would cure all manner of intimate and unmentionable ailments. He was affable, tactful, and reassuring, and the villagers took him to their hearts. He would never want for a friend, or somewhere to stay, or a hot meal, despite the poisonous contents of his bottles. He's one of us, people would say.

The Man Under the Water

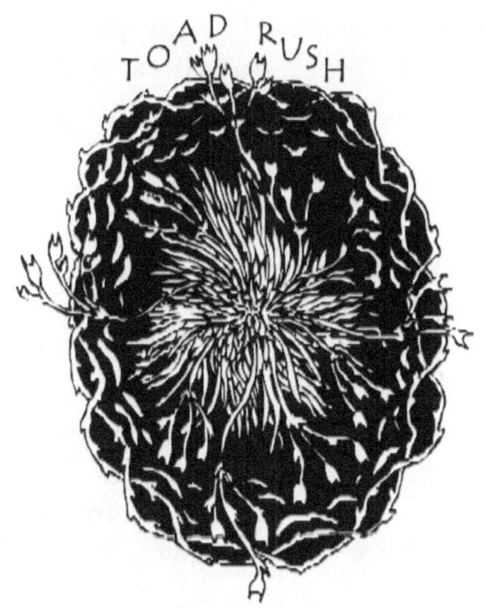

Toad Man

Inspired by the toad rush (*Juncus bufonius*), an unbeautiful, squat little plant with a liking for damp places.

It was rumoured that he could sleep under water. That was nonsense, of course. But he did choose to lurk around the forest pools, and brought with him a light-framed coracle, made of osier-wood and deerskins; he carried it from pool to pool on his back. When he sat down to rest, the coracle crouched with him, and he resembled a giant toad sitting by the water.

This probably was where the rumours started, but you should never underestimate the power of suggestion upon the collective mind of the public. Some were upset at thought of him lurking under the water's surface. When sensible people said 'prove that he does', the silence was deafening. But the suspicions remained. Was he merely a man with a portable boat, or was he truly part toad?

'Come now; no-one can live in a coracle. Surely you would be better off in a little cottage, Toad Man?'

It was kindly meant, but he was irritated. 'I am very happy as I am, my good woman. And don't call me Toad Man. It isn't my name, you know.'

The village woman was thrown into confusion for a moment by his surprisingly refined tone, and then remembered she was talking to a complete ragamuffin.

'Oh. Well. I was thinking you might appreciate it. There is a little ruined cottage in the forest just waiting to be fixed. And don't call me "my good woman".'

'Ah,' said the Toad Man. 'I see we understand one another. I thank you for the thought, but my coracle is all the home I need, and conveniently portable too.'

The bulging of his eyes was so strikingly toad-like that she took a step back.

'But surely,' she said, 'someone like you ...' she almost said a *gentleman* like you but caught herself in time '... someone like you must be accustomed to something more ...'

'Civilised?'

'Yes. No.' She was getting herself into deeper and deeper water. 'It must be bitter cold in the winter.' 'I sleep mostly in the winter. I don't feel it.'

She took this in. He sleeps in the winter, just like a toad. Under that coracle, somewhere near the water.

'But you were gently bred, weren't you? How came you to this?'

'A first son inherits,' said the Toad Man, matter-of-factly. 'A second son goes into the church. I am a seventh son. There was nothing left for me. I built my coracle and made my own life.' He sidled towards her and breathed in her ear. 'I am happy, except that I have no lady to share it. I don't suppose you … ?'

She threw up her hands in horror, as he had known she would. There was no queue forming to be the lady wife of a toad man, even one in possession of his own coracle.

He gave a bubbling, watery chuckle as she rushed off.

The Defiler

Adderstongue

Inspired by the adderstongue fern (*Ophioglossum vulgatum*), a curious plant of meadows and hedgerows.

'You should not have let him in, ma'am,' whispered the maidservant. 'There is something wrong with him.'

The older woman shrugged.

'It's a desperate night. I wouldn't leave a dog out on the doorstep in this.' She jerked her head towards the window – grimy on the inside, rain-streaked on the outside. It seemed that the cottage needed to be turned inside out and cleansed.

'Anyway, he's a vagrant, no more. What is it

that's wrong with him?' The maid glanced at the man snoring by the fire, steam rising from his wet clothes in unfragrant clouds.

'Shush. I don't want to say,' she murmured. 'He might … cast a spell on us. I think he could, you know.'

'*A spell?*'

'Shush, I said. He'll hear us. We must get rid of him. When he's dry. Or when the rain eases. He defiles your hearth, ma'am.' The old woman looked first at her servant, then at the scruffy sleeper. *Defiles* was a strong word. 'Defiles?' she asked. 'How?'

'Did you not hear the hissing in his speech, ma'am?'

'He has an … impediment.' The old woman frowned.

'It's a misfortune. Not a reason to throw someone out into the rain.'

The servant came closer. 'Your eyesight isn'twhat it was, ma'am. But mine is still keen.'

'And?'

'Did you not see?'

'See what?' The old woman was becoming impatient.

'Look closely,' said the maid. 'When he snores, his mouth falls open.' The old woman crept closer, screwed up her eyes and peered at the man.

'Oh! That is unnatural,' she said, pulling back sharply.

The man's open mouth had clearly revealed a pale green forked tongue.

Peddlers and Quacks and Ne'er-do-wells

On the East Wind

Inspired by the wood anemone, or windflower (*Anemone nemorosa*), a spring-flowering plant of old woodlands.

'It began when the wind changed, you know,' said Tam Ullage at the Roundhouse, knowledgeably. 'Not that *I* have cause to complain. Keeps me busy. But that's when they started to turn up.'

This piece of homespun philosophy was soon passed around as unassailable fact. All these odd wanderers had been blown in by the east wind, of course they had. A very stubborn east wind that refused to change. It was as good an explanation as any, and people latched on to it happily. Some of the newcomers were so insubstantial, no more than a cloak and a pair of arms, that it was easy to accept them as mere wind-blown vagrants, unable to resist its steady push or assert their right to head in another direction. The fact that some visitors were the size and substance of a bear and perfectly well able to trudge in any direction they chose, wind or no wind, was overlooked. In the face of an acceptable explanation for this incursion of strangers, that fact was set aside. All these folks have been borne by the wind, just like the strange birds you see after a gale sometimes. Blown off course.

The east wind was an easy entity to blame; it couldn't answer back. And, of course, sooner or later, the wind would change, and all these strangers would be blown away again, vanishing as quickly as they had appeared, prompted, and pushed by the more usual south-westerly. It was a matter of time, nothing more.

Everyone was a little wary of these strangers. It was natural enough. Might they bring disease with them? Might they be on the lookout for things to steal? These were fair questions. The one thing all these wandering folks had in common was that they had no home – or not in the forest anyway. A fixed abode, however humble, gave people a frame of reference; somewhere you were known and could be found, and could be made to answer for any wrongdoing.

This sudden tide of wanderers and passers-through in the forest set the locals exchanging questioning glances.

Unknowns were fine when they came in ones and twos as they usually did. Peddlers and quacks and ne'er-do-wells often stepped out of the trees unannounced, and some of them were welcomed, especially the entertaining ones. But so many all at once? It wasn't natural. And some of them alarmingly odd, too.

Rumour was rife, and waves of unease followed in the wake of the offcomers as they tramped through the woods. They created temporary bivouacs in the church porch and in the shells of ruined cottages as they gathered, one after another.

Even the very birches of the woods showed delicacy of feeling and turned away from these wayfarers, whenever the wind allowed. The forest herself was ill at ease with them.

Of all the villagers, only Leonura the wise woman was unconcerned at the new arrivals. As a matter of fact, she was well pleased.

Leonura raised an eyebrow when people asked about the strangers, and said she knew nothing of it. A bare-faced lie – but she needed to have a care. When you summoned the good and true, the not-so-good would follow, scenting an opportunity. And here they all were. Some were far too stupid to do anything for themselves – the pickers-up of crumbs; some were pretenders and play-actors, accustomed to fooling people occasionally; some had ideas for advancing themselves at the full expense of others; and some were downright evil.

Leonura knew all this, had begun to assess each one to see where they stood on this elastic spectrum, marking them down as dangerous or not. Some, like that viper-tongued creature had worried her, though he had done nothing. It was as well to bear in mind that many of them were not what they seemed – why, she herself was ... No. That thought was banished. After all, some of them might be able to divine what she was thinking.

They were assembling, one by one, in readiness for the meeting at the Hartstongue Inn. But Leonura would have the measure of all of them.

She magicked her husband into a toad and crushed him under her heel.

That was what people said and every one of the strangers knew it. It was as well, was it not, to have a little respect for someone with that sort of reputation?

Part Two

The Herbarium Meets

Contents Part Two

Healers and Herbsters and Hangers-on

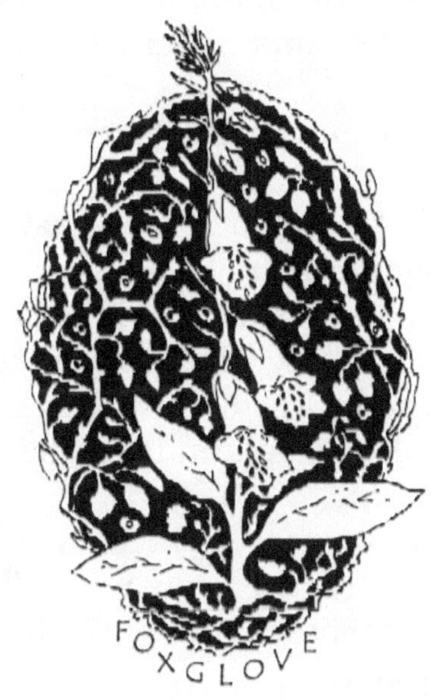

Introducing the Herbarium

Inspired by the foxglove (*Digitalis purpurea*), a plant which provides a wonderful cure for complaints of the heart when properly used. Used improperly, it's usually fatal.

When Leonura stepped into the circle the forest shivered expectantly. The ragbag gathering of people around her shifted from foot to foot, looked over their shoulders, muttered. She had found them at the Hartstongue Inn and chivvied them outside and off intoa clearing. Healers and herbsters and hangers-on, thought Leonura. They all think they have somethingto gain. And so, they have. She took off her gloves andclapped her hands.

'Listen to me and you will learn something to your advantage. Not all of you know each other, so first we will have introductions. I am Leonura, wise woman and herbalist.'

'And witch,' someone muttered. She glared at him.

'Not a witch. Occasional spell-caster, as are some of you. Strictly benign. But let's keep all that between ourselves, shall we?' she said firmly. 'Now then, the rest of you. Let's begin here.' She rapped smartly on the Toad Man's upturned coracle. 'Anybody in?'

The coracle tilted up and its owner emerged blinking into the light.

'I am Alan of Rosworth,' he said, adding resignedly, 'but most of you know me as Toad Man. I sometimes deal in venoms.' And with that he retreated back under the coracle.

'Very well,' said Leonura. 'Toad Man. *Sometimes* deals in venoms. Next.'

Dr Buckler stepped forward, smiling.

'Barabas Buckler, Doctor,' he said, bowing. 'I deal in cures ... sure cures.' Leonura glared at him and his smile slipped away. 'I do no harm,' he added defensively.

'Splendid,' said Leonura. 'Dr Buckler.' She sniffed. 'Does no harm. Next.'

The bearded lady took her turn.

'Ursula Borage,' she said. 'Or Bearded Lady - if you must. I deal in cures for winter ailments. Real cures,' she added, looking pointedly at Dr Buckler, 'not just coloured waters.'

'Welcome, colleague,' said Leonura with obvious respect. 'Ursula Borage. Winter ailments. Next.'

The fork-tongued man edged forward. People stood aside uneasily. 'They call me Adderth-tongue,' he lisped. 'Antidotes for thnakebite. Of courth.' He chuckled unpleasantly.

Leonura nodded. 'Adderstongue. Anti-venom. Next.'

In a ringing voice the monk said, 'I am Stephen of Epping. They call me the Monk because I have the reading and writing. But I am not clergy. I deal in contracts letters and written spells and curses.'

'Stephen of Epping. Literary services,' said Leonura. 'Next.'

The tall, pale woman in violet robes picked her way into the circle.

'Honesty,' she said. 'I do not deal in bottles of coloured water. I foretell the future. Private consultations - expensive,' she added hastily, eying the scruffy group around her. 'I offer moon-healings to those who can afford them.'

'Thank you,' said Leonura. 'Honesty. Seer. Moon-healings. Next.'

A small nervous man tottered forward.

'Knitbone,' he said. 'Broken bones are my speciality. Improvements guaranteed.' He stepped back hastily.

'Mr Knitbone,' said Leonura, a little weary now. 'Breakages fixed. Next.'

'Mercurio,' said the silver-haired man, waving cheerfully. 'You all know me.' He winked. 'Intimate ailments cured.'

'Mercurio,' said Leonura, waving him back again. 'Unmentionables. Next.'

A very ragged man stepped into the circle. 'Timothy Burdock,' he said. 'Baldness cures.'

'You won't be getting any business from me,then,' said the bearded lady, and laughter broke out.

Leonura clapped her hands for silence. 'Mr Burdock. Baldness. Very well. Is that everyone?'

'All except *him*,' said Ursula Borage, nodding towards Old Rustyback, lurking between the trees.

'Come forward, you,' said Leonura.

'They call me Rustyback, on account o' my cloak,' he said. 'I deal in cures, now and then.'

'What he means,' said Dr Buckler, 'is that he buys them cheap from us and sells them on dearer, therogue.'

Rustyback stepped away, shaking his head urgently. 'No sir, not me sir, you are mistaken …'

Leonura intervened. 'Rustyback. *Occasional* dealer in cures.'

He nodded gratefully and sidled away.

'Very well,' said Leonura. 'I'll tell you why you're all here, shall I?'

Cures and Poisons

Sign of the Herbarium

Inspired by the hedge woundwort (*Stachys sylvatica*), a plant that though a little smelly is generally considered good for treating wounds, just like the Herbarium themselves!

'I have a proposition for you all. I'll promise not to poison you, if you'll undertake not to poison me. That's fair, isn't it?'

An uneasy silence followed, until the Toad Man came out of his shell again and said, 'So we all agree not to poison each other? Not even if seriously provoked?'

'That is the idea,' said Leonura patiently. 'Support each other. Like the town guilds.'

It was an invigorating and unusual thought; a healers' guild. Everyone present was clearly wonderingif it could be made to work. They were all in competition with each other, to a degree. And poisoning competitors was not an uncommon means of dealing with the problem.

'So,' said the Toad Man, 'we only poison people who *aren't* in the guild, if they make a nuisance of themselves?'

Honesty stepped forward. 'But I don't go around poisoning people. I don't deal in poisons. I deal in cures.'

'Cures and poisons is one and the same,' said Dr Buckler. 'Just depends on the quantity, don't it?'

Everyone sniggered. It was indeed just a matterof quantity. But they agreed all the same that non-poisoners would be welcome in the new guild, and that the poisoning of those outside it would be an optional activity.

They began to chatter amongst themselves, so Leonura clapped her hands for silence. 'We will call this healers' guild The Herbarium. We will sit down this night and decide on its rules and conditions of membership.' There was unhappy muttering. 'I will provide food for all of you.' The muttering ceased.

The Toad Man had not yet retreated under his coracle. 'I suppose you propose yourself as head of this guild, do you?' he asked Leonura.

'No,' she said. 'I propose my grand-daughter, May.' That girl? The shocked silence lasted a long while.

There were rumours in the village. Odd stories. Tam Ullage at the inn didn't know what to make of them. And Tam, as landlord of the Roundhouse, felt it his natural duty to know what was going on. He prowled the bar, gathering scraps of information as people dropped in. All those healers and quacks and whatnot had deserted his pub and gone to the Hartstongue Inn. That rat-trap! It was unthinkable. Not only that – they had gathered together in the forest afterwards, somebody said, formed a circle, talked gravely. A little later that story had evolved, and the circle had transformed itself into a round table. They had all gathered, taken their place at a round table in the forest. Honest. Not a word of a lie! At each telling the tale was further embroidered; now each healer had appeared in rich clothing, carrying a pennant with a coat of arms.

Tam doubted this entirely. That bunch ofraggedy-bags? Where would they obtain such things? But the reports continued. They had broadswords, and golden helmets with feathers – even the women. Some arrived on white horses with red and gold caparisons.

'Oh, come along, now,' said Tam. 'You can't expect me to believe *that*. We'll be having swords in stones in a minute.'

Bittersweet and Deadly

Secrets Bitter and Sweet

Inspired by the bittersweet, or woody nightshade (*Solanum dulcamara*).

My grandmother Leonura tells me the story. The Herbarium. A group of so-called healers – half of them charlatans from what she says – and I am to lead it! Perhaps she's been too long out in the sun. I shake my head in perplexity. I am miffed that all this has been decided in my absence, without my permission.

'No,' I tell her, 'I don't have the wisdom. They won't listen to me. Surely you must lead. Or Mother.'

'Now, now, young May,' she says, with exaggerated patience, 'have faith. You will find the

wisdom. Your mother can't do it. She isn't capable.
Sometimes the magical skills skip a generation, you
know. And I … well, I am too old to take it on. Besides
there's more. Every last one of them has a secret. That
Rustyback doesn't even know his own secret. Fool.'

I wait.

'I know all the secrets and I will share them with
you. If they step out of line you will have the means to
control them.'

I sense she isn't telling me the truth.

'There's something else, Grandmother, yes?'

'Clever girl,' she says approvingly, tapping her
nose. I wait. 'No,' she says. 'All in good time.'

So, she has a secret, too. And I cannot fathom it.
I've never seen her look so shifty.

*She magicked her husband into a toad and
crushed him under her heel.* That's what they say of her.
She is not a person to be trifled with. So, I don't.

Mercurio, Buckler and Adderstongue

'Let us begin with Mercurio,' says my
grandmother. 'What do you know of him?'

'Mr Mercurio sells …' I hesitate and lower my
eyes modestly. But I need to say it. 'He sells cures for
unfortunate diseases.'

'So he does,' she says, quite matter-of-fact, 'and
how do people catch them?'

I am shocked. This is not a proper subject for a
young woman.

'By breaking their marriage vows.' I say it shyly.
I can't help myself.

'Exactly,' she says. 'If people kept to their marriage vows there'd be a lot less business for Mr M.'

I can't see where she's leading. I am gawping and she takes pity.

'He supports this business with a second enterprise.'

I see the light. 'You mean he sells love potions, too?'

She sighs. I am too slow on the uptake.

'Yes, he does. But he also goes in disguise and arranges discreet introductions and trysts between married persons who ... wish to stray. Do you follow? She looks thoughtfully into the distance. 'So, like many entrepreneurs, he both creates the problem and supplies the solution. Rather ingenious when youconsider it. But I doubt he would like that to be generally known.'

'And Dr Buckler!' I say, eager to show my knowledge. 'Why, *he* sells coloured water and pretends it's a cure. The true healers despise him.'

'Very good,' she says, staring into the distance. I wish she wouldn't do that. It makes me uneasy. 'Very good, but no secret.'

I am deflated again, and grumpy. 'Then what? I suppose he has a third eye in the middle of his forehead, does he?'

My grandmother Leonura turns her unsettling gaze on me, frowning. 'How did you know that?'

'What?' I say, confused. 'I *don't* know that. It's the first thing I thought of, that's all. Anyone can see he has two eyes like anyone else.'

She is very serious now. 'Only the favoured few can see it. Including me. He uses it to transfix people. And he most certainly wouldn't want that fact generally known.'

She gives me a look so piercing I step away from her.

'And what else,' she asks, 'do you see that you haven't seen fit to mention?' She doesn't expect an answer, and I can't offer one.

🕷

'Very well, then,' she says. 'Now what of Adderstongue?'

'Adderstongue?' I simply can't call him "Mr Adderstongue." 'Everyone knows about him. Forked tongue. Pale green. No secret at all.'

'No indeed,' says my grandmother, watching me out of the corner of her eye.

'I suppose he talks to snakes, does he, or turns the milk bad?' I say. Either of these would be damning, never mind the forked tongue.

She catches my drift. 'No, he does not,' she says. 'And the tongue is irrelevant.'

I think that is unlikely.

'But it does worry people, Grandmother.' How could it not?

'Quite so,' she says crisply. 'But he has another secret and guards it well.'

It must be something quite terrible, then, I think.

A smile tugs at the corners of her mouth. 'He does good deeds. Leaves coins behind in the houses of the poor, hides them in the rags of beggars. He won't be able to do it if it's generally known. It's his life's work, and he needs it to be secret. That's the hold you will have over him.'

This is such a surprise it takes me a while to finda sensible answer.

'But surely, Grandmother, you wouldn't want me to put a stop to his generosity?'

'No, of course not. You won't. But he doesn't know that does he? The threat should be enough. Trust me, he won't risk defying you.'

Deadly Secrets

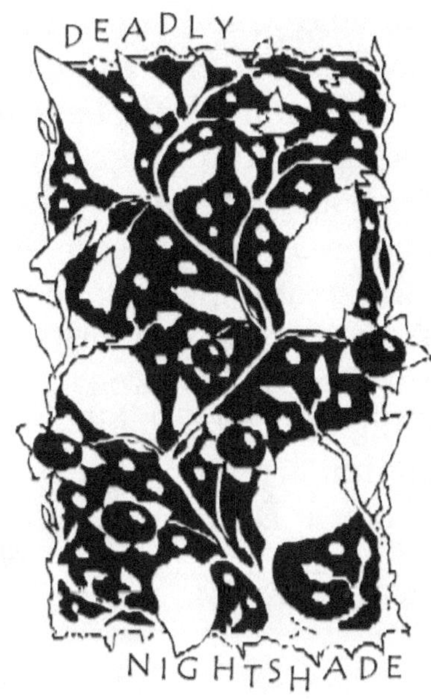

The Monk, Burdock and Rustyback
Inspired by the deadly nightshade (*Atropa belladonna*). No introduction needed.

'As for the monk ...'
'He is not a monk, Grandmother. That is his secret.'
She doesn't like being interrupted.
'How can it be a secret, you idiot, when even *you* know it? No, as for him, he confers with the dead. Don't look at me like that. He can and he does. I'm not entirely convinced he's properly alive himself, to tell the truth. He learned his reading and writing from a deceased abbot who loved books and died in the scriptorium.'

I look sceptical. She shakes her head and goes on. 'The abbot found the hereafter very dull and looked for a mortal to latch onto who would share his passion for the written word. I know this, before you ask, because I have seen the ghost visit our monk. Very easy to conjure up, he is – very partial to an illuminated capital, can't resist them. Very talkative too. Obviously not from a silent order. There's not too many scriveners who take instruction in spelling and page layout from someone who's been dead for a century or more – and I doubt our monk would want people to know about it. Nasty accusations – dealing with the devil – the undead, that sort of thing. Wouldn't do at all. Distinctly bad for business. Just mention Brother Ezekiel to him if he gives you any bother, and he'll see that you know what's what.'

Burdock and Rustyback

'The secrets here are intertwined, as you might say,' says my grandmother. 'And close your mouth before a moth flies in, girl.' I close my mouth. All the things she says make me gape.

She glares at me. 'Tell me what you know, then.'

I know when I'm being set up only to be knocked down again. 'I don't know anything about those two, except Mr Burdock deals in baldness cures.'

'No, no,' she is already losing patience. 'Let me put it simply for you. Mr Burdock follows old Rustyback. He does it discreetly.'

'Why?'

'Because that rusty old cloak contains a hidden cache of gold coins; they fall out one by one as the stitching fails.'

'And Mr Burdock picks them up?'

'Exactly.'

'He wouldn't want Rustyback to know this. That's his secret?'

'Simple enough even for you, my girl. Burdock wears rags, pretends penury, when he has a secret stash of Rustyback's gold.' That is a pretty good secret to know.

'But what of Mr Rustyback? He doesn't know there is gold hidden in the cloak – is that what you're saying?'

'He does not.' She waves her hand airily. I wish she wouldn't. She might cast an accidental spell.

I think it through.

'So, Rustyback has a secret, but he doesn't even know it himself. So, what hold do we have over him?'

'Oh, that. He is a demon condemned to human form.' She says this as if it were an everyday occurrence.

'An incompetent demon, but a demon, nonetheless. Mr Burdock knows this, which is why he follows so stealthily to steal the gold. A demon can turn nasty, you know. In any case, I don't suppose Rustyback would want his demonic nature made public, would he?'

She never ceases to amaze me.

Secrets Deep and Dark

Lords and Ladies. Or not.
Inspired by the lords and ladies (*Arum maculatum*), a poisonous woodland plant.

'As to that Ursula with the beard,' my grandmother says, 'well three husbands is what it's about. All at once. She found one of them on a sea voyage, they say – an inventor, he was. A gent of much brain but very little actual sense. She insisted they should marry, and he caved in. Didn't keep him long, though – got a few useful inventor's secrets out of him and off she went. The second one was a full-blown warlock, by reputation – said she charmed him into marriage, which is hard to believe, looking at her. Wormed a few practical spells out of him – not the silly stuff, you understand – and off she went again. The third one was a doctor of sorts – understood anatomy. She travelled with him after the wedding (which wasn't a real wedding, not with the two other husbands, but he wasn't to know that), and they indulged in a little light grave-robbing. She learned the anatomical trade as they went along, and then said thank you kindly, and disappeared.'

'How do you know all this, Grandmother?' I ask. 'I have my sources, child,' she says, looking shifty. 'The point is she is a shameless bigamist, of which nobody can approve. A woman can be put to death in some parts for that sort of thing – so it is a good secret to know if you need to keep her in line.

'What do you know of the Toad Man?' asks my grandmother.

I'm very quick off the mark this time. 'Why, he is the seventh son on an earl, fallen on hard times. He told the butcher's widow when she went to enquire after his welfare.'

My grandmother smiles. 'Yes. And she told everyone else, including you.'

'So, it's not much of a secret,' I say.

'No, it's not.' She stares out of the window with one of her faraway looks. 'It also isn't true.'

'You mean he isn't a nobleman? Or that the widow lied?' I'm becoming confused now.

My grandmother sighs, not for the first time. 'He is a nobleman, but not the seventh son of an earl – he is an earl himself, and in possession of a great fortune. But he doesn't want it.'

'And earldom and a fortune, and he doesn't want it?' This is inexplicable.

'He likes his life just as it is. No responsibility, no hangers-on begging for money. No demands on his time. Just him and his coracle. It's a secret he'll go to great lengths to keep.'

I begin to understand. I think. 'It'll be easy to keep him in line, then?'

She nods. I marvel at my grandmother's capacity for finding things out.

'How do you know all this?' I ask. But I already know the answer. She has her sources.

Knitbone and Honesty

False Colours

Inspired by the dog violet (*Viola riviniana*). Plants whose names begin with 'dog' are usually those that 'pretend' to be something else - in this case a sweet violet, though it has no scent.

'Mr Knitbone,' says my grandmother, stirring the soup. 'Yes, he is one of the more difficult cases.'

She falls silent, thinking, which is frustrating for me. But I know better than to badger her for more details.

She tastes the soup, thoughtfully. 'What do you notice about him?' she asks.

Ah, I think, this one is going to be a test.

'Well,' I say, 'to begin, he wears odd shoes; one
red, one blue.'

'We won't hold that against him,' she says,
waving the ladle at me. 'Dressing a little strangely
tends to be part of the job for these healers. The colours
are significant. The red is for blood, and the blue is for
bruising. What else?'

I have reached the limits of my observations.

'Does he perhaps turn into a bat at dusk,' I say in
desperation, 'and fly off to a cave in the mountains?'

'You're not taking this very seriously, are you?'
says my grandmother, whacking me on the ear with the
ladle.

There is soup everywhere, in my hair, in my ear.
She doesn't usually waste it like that.

'I'm sorry, Grandmother,' I say, mopping myself
up, 'but I don't know what else to say. Mr Knitbone is
such a transparent character – you can see right
through him. How can he have any secrets?'

She looks at me very keenly. 'Well,' she says at
last, 'that's just it, isn't it? Now you see him, now you
don't. Do you know what a chameleon is?'

'Only Mistress Honesty remains,' I say, 'and
surely she hasn't any shady secrets!' I say it with
complete confidence.

'You shouldn't jump to conclusions based upon a
name,' says my grandmother, knowingly.

I suppress the urge to roll my eyes.

'But surely...'

'Nothing sure about it, child. The first rule of fooling the public is to name a thing the exact opposite of what it is. You'd do well to remember that.'

'But ... she dresses so beautifully, and she sells sound cures – you said so yourself – she had money ...'

'She is a first-class crafty thief,' says my grandmother, not without relish.

'A *thief*? But she has such a good reputation!' I am finding this harder to believe than third eyes, demons and people who blend perfectly into the background.

'I said she was crafty. Good cures, as you say. The ingredients don't come cheap. She sells them at cost price, or near. No-one dresses like that on the pittance they bring in. People trust her because of them, think she's good because she doesn't overcharge, but it's all a front for her top-notch thieving activities. That's where all her money comes from, you see.'

'How do you know?' I am struggling with this. 'I have my sources.'

I really do roll my eyes this time. She sees but pretends not to.

'By the way,' she says, 'don't carry a purse when Honesty's around. She's a very clever pickpocket. And don't drink the wine at the Roundhouse, will you? Tam Ullage drugs it. Makes people – gullible. He sells them things when they're under the influence. That knowledge should be enough to keep him in line, too.'

I only wish I knew what would keep my grandmother in line.

The Pale Man

Inspired by the milk thistle (*Silybum marianum*), a herb much used as a hangover cure.

'There is a road to the north,' said Tam Ullage. 'But you can barely make it out. They don't use it much – or only as far as the bridge, anyway. All overgrown after that. Forest takes it back, see.'

'All overgrown?' said the stranger. 'Sounds about right.'

Tam had a thought.

'If it's that Herb ... Herbar ... the people that sells cures that you're after, you're too late. They've all gone.'

'Mmm,' said the stranger. 'Is that so? No matter.'

Tam's curiosity was piqued. He looked the fellow up and down; strong-looking, tall – but he looked an odd sort of milky colour. Weird, and definitely one of the travelling quacks. What was he doing here if not to join that Herbarium thing? Tam was about to ask, but the stranger got there first.

'I don't like the look of you,' he said.

'Pardon?' said Tam, taken aback.

'You're a very poor colour. Tell me, is your liver doing well, d'ye think?'

Tam hadn't given much consideration to his liver and said so.

'Nobody does,' said the stranger, shaking hishead. 'Nobody does – not til it causes 'em trouble. I've seen it many times. And you, sir, are about to suffer thatsort of trouble, if I'm any judge of it. An occupational hazard, I would suppose.'

'What can I do?' said Tam, horrified that anyone might look askance at his liver.

'Ah, well, as to that, I can be of assistance.' The stranger extracted a small bottle of livid yellow liquid from his bag. 'This will do the trick, and at a most reasonable price, too.'

Tam knew he was being bamboozled – not for the first time – but felt powerless to prevent it. He took the bottle and searched for coins.

'Two bottles is cheaper,' said the stranger.

'Discount for bulk purchase, you know.'
	'How much if I take ten bottles?' asked Tam.
	The stranger narrowed his eyes and then smiled.
'Ah,' he said. 'You are wanting wholesale prices, sir. I
think we understand one another.'

Final Secrets

True Lover's Knot

Inspired by the herb paris (*Paris quadrifolia*), a striking plant of dark woodland places. Also called the true lover's knot.

'They call it the herb paris.' So says my grandmother Leonura, wagging a finger. 'It is an herb of good balance, you see.'

I nod, though I don't see.

'They also call it the true lover's knot.' She wags her finger again. 'Seek it out, young May. It grows in the deep shades and dapples. Find it. Gather it. Weave it into your hat, and you shall meet your true love.'

This is too much.

'Oh, Grandmother! I am not a child. You have taught me many things. But this is what the old wives of the village say. It isn't a spell worthy of you.' Or me, I'm thinking.

She shakes her head in impatience. 'Do you think I don't know a true herb from a false? Now, do as I say. Seek out the plant.' She winks her shrivelled eye. 'Oh, and bring some back for me, too.'

Well, I do as she says. I gather the plant, though I won't wear it. I bring a sprig back for her.

'Small,' she says, looking at it quizzically. 'But it will do.'

And she puts it in her hat and walks off into the coppice. I follow, secretly. What is she doing? She cannot be meeting her true love, I think – she is antique.

But in the clearing she stops. A man, all grey from head to foot glides out to her. She opens her arms to him, and they entwine, forming a true lover's knot. 'I knew you would find me,' she says, smiling, and they melt away into the trees, arm in arm.

It is a long while before I realise she isn't coming back. Oh, Grandmother, what have you done? And who is that pale man?

She magicked her husband into a toad and crushed him under her heel. That's what people used to say of her. *She loved another man, who abetted the crime.*

Could those stories have been true after all? Was the pale man my real grandfather, come back to claim her at last? If it's true, he's taken his time about it. And what happiness can such a pair of old crocks possibly find now? I may never know. It is her final secret.

And what a piece of work she had left for me — The Herbarium. That ragbag of healers. Can I control it? Can I even summon it, as she did? Will it help me or hinder me? I can't tell. But sometimes I think I hear her say in my ear, 'You can, you know.' And yes, I think maybe I can.

May's First Spell

Inspired by the bindweed (*Calystegia sepium*), an indefatigable plant that can find its way anywhere.

The spell flew around the village tangling itself in washing lines, bouncing off walls, narrowly missing chimneys. If it went into the thatch it would be lost forever, and it knew it. So, it swooped low, beneath the eaves, seeking a place of its own, somewhere it could ambush passers-by without any undue expenditure of energy. There must be a space it could own, but it was hard to find, and half an hour later the spell was still pounding itself against wattle and daub like an angry wasp at a window.

And then at last – *at last* – it found a cranny under a lintel and winkled itself inside, gasping. There can be no rest, though, for a spell on a mission, and it

set to work sending out shoots and roots, binding itself
into the fabric of the building, twisting, and anchoring
until it felt secure.

The lintel belonged to the Roundhouse, which
was a very good place for an inquisitive spell. It stood
just above head height and was perfect for reaching out
thin tendrils to probe people's ears, slip into their
mouths, and read their minds. It would report back to
its sender for as long as its strength lasted. All in all, it
was a very workmanlike spell for a newly-fledged wise
woman.

Thus, does nature reclaim her own, all in good time.

The End

www.ingramcontent.com/pod-product-compliance
Lightning Source LLC
Chambersburg PA
CBHW031419200726
48285CB00017BA/2543